Hello, Family Members,

☑ **W9-BMR-172**

Learning to read is one of the most important accomplishments of early childhood. **Hello Reader!** books are designed to help children become skilled readers who like to read. Beginning readers learn to read by remembering frequently used words like "the," "is," and "and"; by using phonics skills to decode new words; and by interpreting picture and text clues. These books provide both the stories children enjoy and the structure they need to read fluently and independently. Here are suggestions for helping your child *before*, *during*, and *after* reading:

Before
- Look at the cover and pictures and have your child predict what the story is about.
- Read the story to your child.
- Encourage your child to chime in with familiar words and phrases.
- Echo read with your child by reading a line first and having your child read it after you do.

During
- Have your child think about a word he or she does not recognize right away. Provide hints such as "Let's see if we know the sounds" and "Have we read other words like this one?"
- Encourage your child to use phonics skills to sound out new words.
- Provide the word for your child when more assistance is needed so that he or she does not struggle and the experience of reading with you is a positive one.
- Encourage your child to have fun by reading with a lot of expression . . . like an actor!

After
- Have your child keep lists of interesting and favorite words.
- Encourage your child to read the books over and over again. Have him or her read to brothers, sisters, grandparents, and even teddy bears. Repeated readings develop confidence in young readers.
- Talk about the stories. Ask and answer questions. Share ideas about the funniest and most interesting characters and events in the stories.

I do hope that you and your child enjoy this book.

—Francie Alexander
 Reading Specialist,
 Scholastic's Learning Ventures

For Wendy, the saver of everything.
Marie, the mind reader.
Tina, my first 4-ever friend.
— J.N.

with love and thanks to
Barbara Seuling
&

Ellen Dreyer	Catherine Nichols
Constance Foland	Roxane Orgill
Marthe Jocelyn	Michele Spirn
Agnes Martinez	Roseann Yaman

Copyright © 2000 by Julia Noonan.
All rights reserved. Published by Scholastic Inc.
SCHOLASTIC, HELLO READER, CARTWHEEL BOOKS and associated logos
are trademarks and/or registered trademarks of Scholastic Inc.

Library of Congress Cataloging-in-Publication Data

Noonan, Julia.
    Hare and Rabbit: Friends Forever / by Julia Noonan.
        p.   cm.—(Hello reader! Level 3)
    "Cartwheel Books."
    Summary: Two friends share cleaning their house, a magic mind-reader
ring, and a bit of jealousy.
    ISBN 0-439-08753-8
    [1. Rabbits—Fiction. 2. Hares—Fiction. 3. Friendship—Fiction.] I. Title:
Hare and Rabbit. II. Title. III. Series.
    PZ7.N74Har   2000
[Fic]—dc21   99-044273

12 11 10 9 8 7 6 5   02 03 04 05

Printed in the U.S.A.   24
First printing, February 2000

Hare and Rabbit

FRIENDS FOREVER

by Julia Noonan

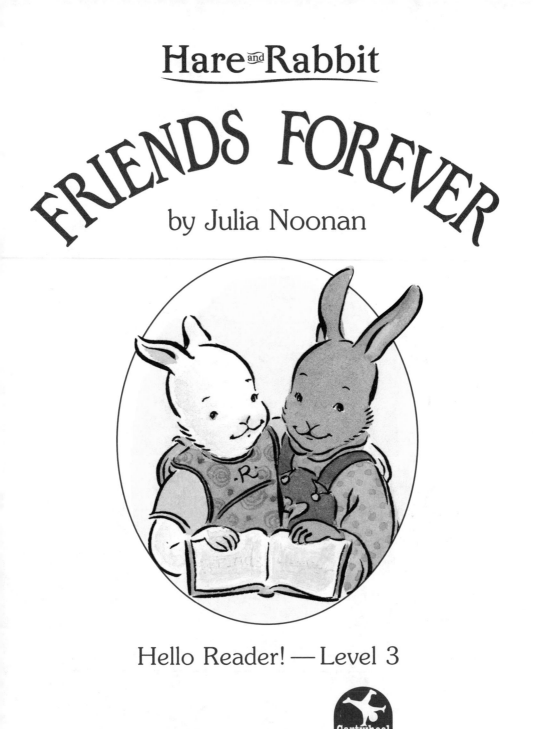

Hello Reader! — Level 3

SCHOLASTIC INC. Cartwheel BOOKS®

New York   Toronto   London   Auckland   Sydney
Mexico City   New Delhi   Hong Kong

Hare and Rabbit
Cleaning House

Hare and Rabbit lived together
in a little house in the woods.

One day, Rabbit picked up an old pair
of garden boots.
"Our house is too messy," she told Hare.
"There is no room for us. We must throw
things away."
"But, Rabbit," said Hare. "We do not know
what things we might need later on."

"We do not need these old newspapers,"
said Rabbit. "And we do not need boots
with holes in them, either."
Rabbit threw them all out the door.

"You're right," said Hare.
She began gathering things to throw
away, too.
"Good-bye, empty shoe box.
Good-bye, dried-up, old paintbrush.
Good-bye, old book with torn pages.
I will miss you!"

Soon a giant pile grew outside the door.
Rabbit threw away a little table
that wiggled.
Then Rabbit looked at the chairs
by the fireplace.
"They are old," she said, pointing
to them.

The inside of the house got emptier and emptier.
"Look!" said Rabbit. "Our house has so much room, I can do cartwheels."

"See how pretty our rug is," said Hare.
"We have not seen it in a long time."
Hare and Rabbit sat on their pretty rug.
"Now what?" asked Hare.
"Now we enjoy our clean house,"
said Rabbit. "We can have tea."

"Good idea," said Hare.
She went to the kitchen.
But she could not find the pot
to make tea.
"Where is the teapot?" asked Hare.
"The teapot had a big chip in it, so
I threw it away," said Rabbit.
"Use a pan instead."
Hare made the tea. She carried it in
on a tray.
"Where should I put it?" asked Hare.
"Set it on the floor, I guess," said Rabbit.

"I miss the little table that wiggled,"
said Hare.
"Where is my cup?" asked Rabbit.
"It had a chip in it, too," said Hare.
She poured the tea.
"It does not feel right having tea on
the floor without my cup," said Rabbit.
"And I miss my chair."
"I miss a lot of things," said Hare.
Hare looked at Rabbit.
Rabbit looked at Hare.
Together, they went outside.

It was dark when they were done
putting everything back in its place.
Hare put the tray on the little table
that wiggled. Then she poured the tea.
"It feels so cozy having all of our things
around us again," she said.

"You are so right," said Rabbit.
"If we want to do cartwheels,
we can always do them outside." ❖

Hare and Rabbit
Mind-Reader Ring

One morning Hare sat down
to breakfast.
Rabbit was already at the table.
"Where is the prize from the new
box of cereal?" asked Hare, peeking
into the box.

"I already have it," said Rabbit.
"What is it?" asked Hare.
"It is a magic mind-reader ring,"
said Rabbit. "Now I know everything
you are thinking."

"Can you tell me what I am
thinking right now?" asked Hare.
"Yes," said Rabbit. "You're thinking
that you wish you got the ring."
"You're right," said Hare.

Hare walked out of the kitchen
into the living room.
She called back to Rabbit.
"Can you tell me what I am thinking now?"
"Yes," said Rabbit. "You're wondering
if I can read your mind when you are in
a different room."

"Oh, dear!" said Hare, as she walked back into the kitchen. "You *do* know what I'm thinking."
"Of course," said Rabbit. "Now think of something else."
Hare thought, *I do not like Rabbit reading my mind.*

Rabbit said, "You're thinking about
which kind of cereal to eat. Am I right?"
Hare felt much better.
"Right again!" said Hare.
"Really?" asked Rabbit.
"Really," said Hare.

Hare smiled as she put cereal in her bowl.
Hare thought, *I love Carrot Crunch
cereal.* "And what am I thinking now?"
asked Hare.
"You're trying to decide if you want juice
or tea," said Rabbit.

"Oh, Rabbit. You're so clever," said Hare. "Perhaps we should hang out a sign that says, 'Mind-Reader Rabbit the Great lives here.'"

"Do you think that is a good idea?" asked Rabbit.
"Yes," said Hare. "And I will be your helper, in a beautiful costume. I can't wait. I'm going to make the sign right now. It will tell the *whole world* you can read minds."

"The *whole world*?" said Rabbit.
"Yes," said Hare. "Everyone will come.
You will read all of their minds."
"Wait a minute," said Rabbit.
"The ring feels very strange. I think it
may be losing its power."
"Give me the ring," said Hare.

Rabbit gave Hare the ring.
Hare tried it on. "You're right," she said,
taking it off again.
"The ring has lost its power. But I bet
I know what you are thinking anyway."
"What?" asked Rabbit.
"That it's time to eat," said Hare. ❖

Hare and Rabbit
Boo-Boo Bunny

"Look!" said Rabbit. "A letter has come from my old friend Boo-Boo."

Hare's long ears stood straight up.
"You never told me you had a friend
named Boo-Boo."
"I knew her a long time ago," said Rabbit.
"We used to work together at the circus."

Rabbit opened the envelope
and read the card inside.
"Great news!" she said. "Boo-Boo
is riding bareback in a circus that
is coming to our town."
Rabbit held up two tickets.
"We're invited to join her
under the Big Top."

Rabbit handed Hare the card.
One side had a picture and said:

*Boo-Boo Bunny
Bareback Ballerina!*

"She looks like a very fancy bunny,"
said Hare.
Hare turned the card over.
The other side said:

*See you at the circus!
Love, Boo-Boo*

Hare thought to herself: *Boo-Boo . . .
what a silly name.*
"We better hurry," said Rabbit suddenly.
"The circus is today!"

The stands were full when Hare
and Rabbit got to the circus.
The clowns were doing silly tricks.

Then out came the horses into the ring.
With them came a beautiful bunny.
She wore fancy, sparkling clothes.
She had feathers in her hair
and satin slippers on her feet.
"It's Boo-Boo!" said Rabbit.

Everyone cheered as Boo-Boo
did her tricks.
She jumped from horse to horse,
and off and on again.
"That doesn't look so very hard to do,"
said Hare quietly.
"Look at her," said Rabbit. "She is the
best bareback rider anywhere!"
"She looks like a show-off to me,"
said Hare.

When the circus was over, Rabbit said
to Hare, "Did you like the show?"
"Yes, I did," said Hare. "But I would not
call a bunny who jumps on horses
a ballerina."
Hare and Rabbit walked toward
Boo-Boo's circus wagon.

When they reached the wagon,
Boo-Boo was waiting.
She did not look so fancy now
without her costume.

After Boo-Boo and Rabbit hugged hello,
Rabbit smiled at Hare.
"Boo-Boo," said Rabbit, "I want you
to meet my very best friend." ❖